SIGNATURE SERIES

# TEXTS FOR NOTHING

## Samuel Beckett

*Translated from the original French by the author*

CALDER & BOYARS

LONDON

First published in 1974 by Calder and Boyars Ltd.
18, Brewer Street, London W1R 4AS

Originally published in *Nouvelles et Textes pour Rien*
by Editions de Minuit, Paris, 1954. Original English
text published in *No's Knife* by Calder and Boyars, 1967.

ISBN 0 7145 0984 1

Printed in Great Britain by
Whitstable Litho, Straker Brothers Ltd

# TEXTS FOR NOTHING

# TEXTS FOR NOTHING

# I

Suddenly, no, at last, long last, I couldn't any more, I couldn't go on. Someone said, You can't stay here. I couldn't stay there and I couldn't go on. I'll describe the place, that's unimportant. The top, very flat, of a mountain, no, a hill, but so wild, so wild, enough. Quag, heath up to the knees, faint sheeptracks, troughs scooped deep by the rains. It was far down in one of these I was lying, out of the wind. Glorious prospect, but for the mist that blotted out everything, valleys, loughs, plain and sea. How can I go on, I shouldn't have begun, no, I had to begin. Someone said, perhaps the same, What possessed you to come? I could have stayed in my den, snug and dry, I couldn't. My den, I'll describe it, no, I can't. It's simple, I can do nothing any more, that's what you think. I say to the body, Up with you now, and I can feel it struggling, like an old hack foundered in the street, struggling no more, struggling again, till it gives up. I say to the head, Leave it alone, stay quiet, it stops breathing, then pants on worse than ever. I am far from all that wrangle, I shouldn't bother with it, I need nothing, neither to go on nor to stay where I am, it's truly all one to me, I should turn away from it all, away from the body, away from the head, let them work it out between them, let them cease, I can't, it's I would have to cease. Ah yes, we seem to be more than one, all deaf, not even, gathered together for life. Another said, or the same, or the first, they all have the same voice, the same ideas, All you had to do was stay at home. Home. They wanted me to go home. My dwelling-place. But for the mist, with good eyes, with a telescope, I could see it from here. It's not just tiredness, I'm not just tired, in spite of the climb. It's not that I want to stay here either. I had heard tell, I must have heard tell of the view, the distant sea in hammered lead, the so-called golden vale so often sung, the double valleys, the glacial loughs, the city in its haze, it was all on every tongue. Who are these people anyway? Did they follow me up here, go before me, come with me? I am down in the hole the centuries have dug, centuries of filthy weather, flat on my face on the dark earth sodden with the creeping saffron waters it slowly drinks. They are up above, all round me, as in a graveyard. I can't raise my eyes to them, what a pity, I wouldn't see their faces, their legs perhaps, plunged in the heath. Do they see me, what can they see of me? Perhaps there is no one left, perhaps they are all gone, sickened. I listen and it's the same thoughts I hear, I mean the same as ever, strange. To think in the valley the sun is blazing all down the ravelled sky. How long have I been here, what a question, I've often wondered. And often I could answer, An hour, a month, a year, a century, depending on what I meant by here, and me, and being, and there I never went looking for extravagant meanings, there I never much varied, only the here would sometimes seem to vary. Or I said, I can't have been here long, I wouldn't have held out. I hear the curlews, that means close of day, fall of night, for that's the way with curlews, silent all day, then crying when the darkness gathers, that's the way with those wild creatures and so short-lived, compared with me. And that other question I know so well too, What possessed you to come?, unanswerable, so that I answered, To change, or, It's not me, or, Chance, or again, To see, or again, years of great sun, Fate, I feel that other coming, let it come, it won't catch me napping. All is noise, unending suck of black sopping peat, surge of giant ferns, heathery gulfs of quiet where the wind drowns, my life and its old jingles. To change, to see, no, there's no more to see, I've seen it all, till my eyes are blear, nor to get away from harm, the harm is done, one day the harm was done, the day my feet dragged me out that must go their ways, that I let go their ways and drag me here, that's what possessed me to come. And what I'm doing, all-important, breathing in and out and saying, with words like smoke, I can't go, I can't stay, let's see what happens next. And in the way of sensation? My God I can't complain, it's himself all right, only muffled, like buried in snow, less the warmth, less the drowse, I can follow them well, all the voices, all the parts, fairly well, the cold is eating me, the wet too, at least I presume so, I'm far. My rheumatism in any case is no more than a memory, it hurts me no more than my mother's did, when it hurt her. Eye ravening patient in the haggard vulture face, perhaps it's carrion time. I'm up there and I'm down here, under my gaze, foundered, eyes closed, ear cupped against the sucking peat, we're of one mind, all of one mind, always were, deep down, we're fond of one another, we're sorry for one another, but there it is, there's nothing we can do for one another. One thing at least is certain, in an hour it will be too late, in half-an-hour it will be night, and yet it's not, not certain, what is not certain, absolutely certain, that night prevents what day permits, for those who know how to go about it, who have the will to go about it, and the strength, the strength to try again. Yes, it will be night, the mist will clear, I know my mist, for all my distraction, the wind freshen and the whole nightsky open over the mountain, with its lights, including the Bears, to guide me once again on my way, let's wait for night. All mingles, times and tenses, at first I only had been here, now I'm here still, soon I won't be here yet, toiling up the slope, or in the bracken by the wood, it's larch, I don't try to understand, I'll never try to understand any more, that's what you think, for the moment I'm here, always have been, always shall be, I won't be afraid of the big words any more, they are not big. I don't remember coming, I can't go, all my little company, my eyes are closed and I feel the wet humus harsh against my cheek, my hat is gone, it can't be gone far, or the wind has swept it away, I was attached to it. Sometimes it's the sea, other times the mountains, often it was the forest, the city, the plain too, I've flirted with the plain too, I've given myself up for dead all over the place, of hunger, of old age, murdered, drowned, and then for no reason, of tedium, nothing like breathing your last to put new life in you, and then the rooms, natural death, tucked up in bed, smothered in household gods, and always muttering, the same old mutterings, the same old stories, the same old questions and answers, no malice in me, hardly any, stultior stultissimo, never an imprecation, not such a fool, or else it's gone from mind. Yes, to the end, always muttering, to lull me and keep me company, and all ears always, all ears for the old stories, as when my father took me on his knee and read me the one about Joe Breem, or Breen, the son of a lighthouse keeper, evening after evening, all the long winter through. A tale, it was a tale for children, it all happened on a rock, in the storm, the mother was dead and the gulls came beating against the light, Joe jumped into the sea, that's all I remember, a knife between his teeth, did what was to be done and came back, that's all I remember this evening, it ended happily, it began unhappily and it ended happily, every evening, a comedy, for children. Yes, I was my father and I was my son, I asked myself questions and answered as best I could, I had it told to me evening after evening, the same old story I knew by heart and couldn't believe, or we walked together, hand in hand, silent, sunk in our worlds, each in his worlds, the hands forgotten in each other. That's how I've held out till now. And this evening again it seems to be working, I'm in my arms, I'm holding myself in my arms, without much tenderness, but faithfully, faithfully. Sleep now, as under that ancient lamp, all twined together, tired out with so much talking, so much listening, so much toil and play.

## II

Above is the light, the elements, a kind of light, sufficient to see by, the living find their ways, without too much trouble, avoid one another, unite, avoid the obstacles, without too much trouble, seek with their eyes, close their eyes, halting, without halting, among the elements, the living. Unless it has changed, unless it has ceased. The things too must still be there, a little more worn, a little even less, many still standing where they stood in the days of their indifference. Here you are under a different glass, not long habitable either, it's time to leave it. You are there, there it is, where you are will never long be habitable. Go then, no, better stay, for where would you go, now that you know? Back above? There are limits. Back in that kind of light. See the cliffs again, be again between the cliffs and the sea, reeling shrinking with your hands over your ears, headlong, innocent, suspect, noxious. Seek, by the excessive light of night, a demand commensurate with the offer, and go to ground empty-handed at the old crack of day. See Mother Calvet again, creaming off the garbage before the nightmen come. She must still be there. With her dog and her skeletal baby-buggy. What could be more endurable? She wavered through the night, a kind of trident in her hand, muttering and ejaculating, Your highness! Your honour! The dog tottered on its hindlegs begging, hooked its paws over the rim of the can and snouted round with her in the muck. It got in her way,

Loan Receipt
Liverpool John Moores University
Library Services

Borrower Name: Hughes,Bethan
Borrower ID: **********8164

Texts for nothing /
31111000710010
Due Date: 26/09/2014 23:59

Total Items: 1
23/07/2014 10:32

Please keep your receipt in case of
dispute.

she cursed it for a lousy cur and let it have its way. There's a good memory. Mother Calvet. She knew what she liked, perhaps even what she would have liked. And beauty, strength, intelligence, the latest, daily, action, poetry, all one price for one and all. If only it could be wiped from knowledge. To have suffered under that miserable light, what a blunder. It let nothing show, it would have gone out, nothing terrible, nothing showed, of the true affair, it would have snuffed out. And now here, what now here, one enormous second, as in Paradise, and the mind slow, slow, nearly stopped. And yet it's changing, something is changing, it must be in the head, slowly in the head the ragdoll rotting, perhaps we're in a head, it's as dark as in a head before the worms get at it, ivory dungeon. The words too, slow, slow, the subject dies before it comes to the verb, words are stopping too. Better off then than when life was babble? That's it, that's it, the bright side. And the absence of others, does that count for so little? Pah others, that's nothing, others never inconvenienced anyone, and there must be a few here too, other others, invisible, mute, what does it matter. It's true you hid from them, hugged their walls, true, you miss that here, you miss the derivatives, here it's pure ache, pah you were saying that above and you a living mustard-plaster. So long as the words keep coming nothing will have changed, there are the old words out again. Utter, there's nothing else, utter, void yourself of them, here as always, nothing else. But they are failing, true, that's the change, they are failing, that's bad, bad. Or it's the dread of coming to the last, of having said all, your all, before the end, no, for that will be the end, the end of all, not certain. To need to groan and not be able, Jesus, better ration yourself, watch out for the genuine deathpangs, some are deceptive, you think you're home, start howling and revive, health-giving howls, better be silent, it's the only method, if you want to end, not a word but smiles, end rent with stifled imprecations, burst with speechlessness, all is possible, what now. Perhaps above it's summer, a summer Sunday, Mr Joly is in the belfry, he has wound up the clock, now he's ringing the bells. Mr Joly. He had only one leg and a half. Sunday. It was folly to be abroad. The roads were crawling with them, the same roads so often kind. Here at least none of that, no talk of a creator and nothing very definite in the way of a creation. Dry, it's possible, or wet, or slime, as before matter took ill. Is this stuff air that permits you to suffocate still, almost audibly at times, it's possible, a kind of air. What exactly is going on, exactly, ah old xanthic laugh, no, farewell mirth, good riddance, it was never droll. No, but one more memory, one last memory, it may help, to abort again. Piers pricking his oxen o'er the plain, no, for at the end of the furrow, before turning to the next, he raised his eyes to the sky and said, Bright again too early. And sure enough, soon after, the snow. In other words the night was black, when it fell at last, but no, strange, it wasn't, in spite of the buried sky. The way was long that led back to the den, over the fields, a winding way, it must still be there. When it comes to the top of the cliff it springs, some might think blindly, but no, wilily, like a goat, in hairpin zigzags towards the shore. Never had the sea so thundered from afar, the sea beneath the snow, though superlatives have lost most of their charm. The day had not been fruit-ful, as was only natural, considering the season, that of the very last leeks. It was none the less the return, to what no matter, the return, unscathed, always a matter for wonder. What happened? Is that the question? An encounter? Bang! No. Level with the farm of the Graves brothers a brief halt, opposite the lamplit window. A glow, red, afar, at night, in winter, that's worth having, that must have been worth having. There, it's done, it ends there, I end there. A far memory, far from the last, it's possible, the legs seem to be still working. A pity hope is dead. No. How one hoped above, on and off. With what diversity.

# III

Leave, I was going to say leave all that. What matter who's speaking, someone said what matter who's speaking. There's going to be a departure, I'll be there, I won't miss it, it won't be me, I'll be here, I'll say I'm far from here, it won't be me, I won't say anything, there's going to be a story, someone's going to try and tell a story. Yes, no more denials, all is false, there is no one, it's understood, there is nothing, no more phrases, let us be dupes, dupes of every time and tense, until it's done, all past and done, and the voices cease, it's only voices, only lies. Here, depart from here and go elsewhere, or stay here, but coming and going. Start by stirring, there must be a body, as of old, I don't deny it, no more denials, I'll say I'm a body, stirring back and forth, up and down, as required. With a cluther of limbs and organs, all that is needed to live again, to hold out a little time, I'll call that living, I'll say it's me, I'll get standing, I'll stop thinking, I'll be too busy, getting standing, staying standing, stirring about, holding out, getting to tomorrow, tomorrow week, that will be ample, a week will be ample, a week in spring, that puts the jizz in you. It's enough to will it, I'll will it, will me a body, will me a head, a little strength, a little courage, I'm starting now, a week is soon served, then back here, this inextricable place, far from the days, the far days, it's not going to be easy. And why, come to think, no no, leave it, no more of that, don't listen to it all, don't say it all, it's all old, all one, once and for all. There you are now on your feet, I give you my word, I swear they're yours, I swear it's mine, get to work with your hands, palp your skull, seat of the understanding, without which nix, then the rest, the lower regions, you'll be needing them, and say what you're like, have a guess, what kind of man, there has to be a man, or a woman, feel between your legs, no need of beauty, nor of vigour, a week's a short stretch, no one's going to love you, don't be alarmed. No, not like that, too sudden, I gave myself a start. And to start with stop palpitating, no one's going to kill you, no one's going to love you and no one's going to kill you, perhaps you'll emerge in the high depression of Gobi, you'll feel at home there. I'll wait for you here, no, I'm alone, I alone am, this time it's I must go. I know how I'll do it, I'll be a man, there's nothing else for it, a kind of man, a kind of old tot, I'll have a nanny, I'll be her sweet pet, she'll give me her hand, to cross over, she'll let me loose in the Green, I'll be good, I'll sit quiet as a mouse in a corner and comb my beard, I'll tease it out, to look more bonny, a little more bonny, if only it could be like that. She'll say to me, Come, doty, it's time for bye-bye. I'll have no responsibility, she'll have all the responsibility, her name will be Bibby, I'll call her Bibby, if only it could be like that. Come, ducky, it's time for yum-yum. Who taught me all I know, I alone, in the old wanderyears, I deduced it all from nature, with the help of an all-in-one, I know it's not me, but it's too late now, too late to deny it, the knowledge is there, the bits and scraps, flickering on and off, turn about, winking on the storm, in league to fool me. Leave it and go, it's time to go, to say so anyway, the moment has come, it's not known why. What matter how you describe yourself, here or

17

elsewhere, fixed or mobile, without form or oblong like man, in the dark or the light of the heavens, I don't know, it seems to matter, it's not going to be easy. And if I went back to where all went out and on from there, no, that would lead nowhere, never led anywhere, the memory of it has gone out too, a great flame and then blackness, a great spasm and then no more weight or traversable space. I tried throwing me off a cliff, collapsing in the street in the midst of mortals, that led nowhere, I gave up. Take the road again that cast me up here, then retrace it, or follow it on, wise advice. That's so that I'll never stir again, dribble on here till time is done, murmuring every ten centuries, It's not me, it's not true, it's not me, I'm far. No no, I'll speak now of the future, I'll speak in the future, as when I used to say, in the night, to myself, Tomorrow I'll put on my dark blue tie, with the yellow stars, and put it on, when night was past. Quick quick before I weep. I'll have a crony, my own vintage, my own bog, a fellow warrior, we'll relive our campaigns and compare our scratches. Quick quick. He'll have served in the navy, perhaps under Jellicoe, while I was potting at the invader from behind a barrel of Guinness, with my arquebuse. We have not long, that's the spirit, in the present, not long to live, it's our positively last winter, halleluiah. We wonder what will carry us off in the end. He's gone in the wind, I in the prostate rather. We envy each other, I envy him, he envies me, occasionally. I catheterize myself, unaided, with trembling hand, bent double in the public pisshouse, under cover of my cloak, people take me for a dirty old man. He waits for me to finish, sitting on a bench, coughing up his guts, spitting into a snuffbox which no sooner overflows than he empties it in the canal, out of civic-mindedness. We have well deserved of our motherland, she'll get us into the Incurables before we die. We spend our life, it's ours, trying to bring together in the same instant a ray of sunshine and a free bench, in some oasis of public verdure, we've been seized by a love of nature, in our sere and yellow, it belongs to one and all, in places. In a choking murmur he reads out to me from the paper of the day before, he had far far better been the blind one. The sport of kings is our passion, the dogs too, we have no political opinions, simply limply republican. But we also have a soft spot for the Windsors, the Hanoverians, I forget, the Hohenzollerns is it. Nothing human is foreign to us, once we have digested the racing news. No, alone, I'd be better off alone, it would be quicker. He'd nourish me, he had a friend a pork-butcher, he'd ram the ghost back down my gullet with black pudding. With his consolations, allusions to cancer, recollections of imperishable raptures, he'd prevent discouragement from sapping my foundations. And I, instead of concentrating on my own horizons, which might have enabled me to throw them under a lorry, would let my mind be taken off them by his. I'd say to him, Come on, gunner, leave all that, think no more about it, and it's I would think no more about it, besotted with brotherliness. And the obligations! I have in mind particularly the appointments at ten in the morning, hail rain or shine, in front of Duggan's, thronged already with sporting men fevering to get their bets out of harm's way before the bars open. We were, there we are past and gone again, so much the better, so much the better, most punctual I must say. To see the remains of Vincent arriving in sheets of rain, with the brave involuntary swagger of the old tar, his head swathed in a bloody clout and a glitter in his eye, was for the acute observer an example of what man is capable of, in his pursuit of pleasure. With one hand he sustained his sternum, with the heel of the other his spinal column, as if tempted to break into a hornpipe, no, that's all memories, last shifts older than the flood. See what's happening here, where there's no one, where nothing happens, get something to happen here, someone to be here, then put an end to it, have silence, get into silence, or another sound, a sound of other voices than those of life and death, of lives and deaths everyone's but mine, get into my story in order to get out of it, no, that's all meaningless. Is it possible I'll sprout a head at last, all my very own, in which to brew poisons worthy of me, and legs to kick my heels with, I'd be there at last, I could go at last, it's all I ask, no, I can't ask anything. Just the head and the two legs, or one, in the middle, I'd go hopping. Or just the head, nice and round, nice and smooth, no need of lineaments, I'd go rolling, downhill, almost a pure spirit, no, that wouldn't work, all is uphill from here, the leg is unavoidable, or the equivalent, perhaps a few annular joints, contractile, great ground to be covered with them. To set out from Duggan's door, on a spring morning of rain and shine, not knowing if you'll ever get to evening, what's wrong with that? It would be so easy. To be bedded in that flesh or in another, in that arm held by a friendly hand, and in that hand, without arms, without hands, and without soul in those trembling souls, through the crowd, the hoops, the toy balloons, what's wrong with that? I don't know, I'm here, that's all I know, and that it's still not me, it's of that the best has to be made. There is no flesh anywhere, nor any way to die. Leave all that, to want to leave all that, not knowing what that means, all that, it's soon said, soon done, in vain, nothing has stirred, no one has spoken. Here, nothing will happen here, no one will be here, for many a long day. Departures, stories, they are not for tomorrow. And the voices, wherever they come from, have no life in them.

# IV

Where would I go, if I could go, who would I be, if I could be, what would I say, if I had a voice, who says this, saying it's me? Answer simply, someone answer simply. It's the same old stranger as ever, for whom alone accusative I exist, in the pit of my inexistence, of his, of ours, there's a simple answer. It's not with thinking he'll find me, but what is he to do, living and bewildered, yes, living, say what he may. Forget me, know me not, yes, that would be the wisest, none better able than he. Why this sudden affability after such desertion, it's easy to understand, that's what he says, but he doesn't understand. I'm not in his head, nowhere in his old body, and yet I'm there, for him I'm there, with him, hence all the confusion. That should have been enough for him, to have found me absent, but it's not, he wants me there, with a form and a world, like him, in spite of him, me who am everything, like him who is nothing. And when he feels me void of existence it's of his he would have me void, and vice versa, mad, mad, he's mad. The truth is he's looking for me to kill me, to have me dead like him, dead like the living. He knows all that, but it's no help his knowing it, I don't know it, I know nothing. He protests he doesn't reason and does nothing but reason, crooked, as if that could improve matters. He thinks words fail him, he thinks because words fail him he's on his way to my speechlessness, to being speechless with my speechlessness, he would like it to be my

fault that words fail him, of course words fail him.
He tells his story every five minutes, saying it is not his,
there's cleverness for you. He would like it to be my
fault that he has no story, of course he has no story,
that's no reason for trying to foist one on me. That's
how he reasons, wide of the mark, but wide of what
mark, answer us that. He has me say things saying it's
not me, there's profundity for you, he has me who say
nothing say it's not me. All that is truly crass. If at
least he would dignify me with the third person, like
his other figments, not he, he'll be satisfied with
nothing less than me, for his me. When he had me,
when he was me, he couldn't get rid of me quick
enough, I didn't exist, he couldn't have that, that
was no kind of life, of course I didn't exist, any more
than he did, of course it was no kind of life, now he
has it, his kind of life, let him lose it, if he wants to be
in peace, with a bit of luck. His life, what a mine,
what a life, he can't have that, you can't fool him,
ergo it's not his, it's not him, what a thought, treat
him like that, like a vulgar Molloy, a common Malone,
those mere mortals, happy mortals, have a heart, land
him in that shit, who never stirred, who is none but
me, all things considered, and what things, and how
considered, he had only to keep out of it. That's how
he speaks, this evening, how he has me speak, how he
speaks to himself, how I speak, there is only me, this
evening, here, on earth, and a voice that makes no
sound because it goes towards none, and a head strewn
with arms laid down and corpses fighting fresh, and a
body, I nearly forgot. This evening, I say this evening, perhaps it's morning. And all these things, what
things, all about me, I won't deny them any more,
there's no sense in that any more. If it's nature perhaps
it's trees and birds, they go together, water and air,

so that all may go on, I don't need to know the details, perhaps I'm sitting under a palm. Or it's a room, with furniture, all that's required to make life comfortable, dark, because of the wall outside the window. What am I doing, talking, having my figments talk, it can only be me. Spells of silence too, when I listen, and hear the local sounds, the world sounds, see what an effort I make, to be reasonable. There's my life, why not, it is one, if you like, if you must, I don't say no, this evening. There has to be one, it seems, once there is speech, no need of a story, a story is not compulsory, just a life, that's the mistake I made, one of the mistakes, to have wanted a story for myself, whereas life alone is enough. I'm making progress, it was time, I'll learn to keep my foul mouth shut before I'm done, if nothing foreseen crops up. But he who somehow comes and goes, unaided from place to place, even though nothing happens to him, true, what of him? I stay here, sitting, if I'm sitting, often I feel sitting, sometimes standing, it's one or the other, or lying down, there's another possibility, often I feel lying down, it's one of the three, or kneeling. What counts is to be in the world, the posture is immaterial, so long as one is on earth. To breathe is all that is required, there is no obligation to ramble, or receive company, you may even believe yourself dead on condition you make no bones about it, what more liberal regimen could be imagined, I don't know, I don't imagine. No point under such circumstances in saying I am somewhere else, someone else, such as I am I have all I need to hand, for to do what, I don't know, all I have to do, there I am on my own again at last, what a relief that must be. Yes, there are moments, like this moment, when I seem almost restored to the feasible. Then it goes, all goes, and I'm far again, with a far story again, I wait for me afar for my story to begin, to end, and again this voice cannot be mine. That's where I'd go, if I could go, that's who I'd be, if I could be.

# V

I'm the clerk, I'm the scribe, at the hearings of what cause I know not. Why want it to be mine, I don't want it. There it goes again, that's the first question this evening. To be judge and party, witness and advocate, and he, attentive, indifferent, who sits and notes. It's an image, in my helpless head, where all sleeps, all is dead, not yet born, I don't know, or before my eyes, they see the scene, the lids flicker and it's in. An instant and then they close again, to look inside the head, to try and see inside, to look for me there, to look for someone there, in the silence of quite a different justice, in the toils of that obscure assize where to be is to be guilty. That is why nothing appears, all is silent, one is frightened to be born, no, one wishes one were, so as to begin to die. One, meaning me, it's not the same thing, in the dark where I will in vain to see there can't be any willing. I could get up, take a little turn, I long to, but I won't. I know where I'd go, I'd go into the forest, I'd try and reach the forest, unless that's where I am, I don't know where I am, in any case I stay. I see what it is, I seek to be like the one I seek, in my head, that my head seeks, that I bid my head seek, with its probes, within itself. No, don't pretend to seek, don't pretend to think, just be vigilant, the eyes staring behind the lids, the ears straining for a voice not from without, were it only to sound an instant, to tell another lie. I hear, that must be the voice of reason again, that the vigil is in vain, that I'd be better advised to take a little turn, the way you manoeuvre a tin soldier. And no doubt it's the same voice answers that I can't, I who but a moment ago seemed to think I could, unless it's old shuttlecock sentiment chiming in, full stop, got all that. Why did Pozzo leave home, he had a castle and retainers. Insidious question, to remind me I'm in the dock. Sometimes I hear things that seem for a moment judicious, for a moment I'm sorry they are not mine. Then what a relief, what a relief to know I'm mute for ever, if only it didn't distress me. And deaf, it seems to me sometimes that deaf I'd be less distressed, at being mute, listen to that, what a relief not to have that on my conscience. Ah yes, I hear I have a kind of conscience, and on top of that a kind of sensibility, I trust the orator is not forgetting anything, and without ceasing to listen or drive the old quill I'm afflicted by them, I heard, it's noted. This evening the session is calm, there are long silences when all fix their eyes on me, that's to make me fly off my hinges, I feel on the brink of shrieks, it's noted. Out of the corner of my eye I observe the writing hand, all dimmed and blurred by the—by the reverse of farness. Who are all these people, gentlemen of the long robe, according to the image, but according to it alone, there are others, there will be others, other images, other gentlemen. Shall I never see the sky again, never be free again to come and go, in sunshine and in rain, the answer is no, all answer no, it's well I didn't ask anything, that's the kind of extravagance I envy them, till the echoes die away. The sky, I've heard—the sky and earth, I've heard great accounts of them, now that's pure word for word, I invent nothing. I've noted, I must have noted many a story with them as setting, they create the atmosphere.

Between them where the hero stands a great gulf is fixed, while all about they flow together more and more, till they meet, so that he finds himself as it were under glass, and yet with no limit to his movements in all directions, let him understand who can, that is no part of my attributions. The sea too, I am conversant with the sea too, it belongs to the same family, I have even gone to the bottom more than once, under various assumed names, don't make me laugh, if only I could laugh, all would vanish, all what, who knows, all, me, it's noted. Yes, I see the scene, I see the hand, it comes creeping out of shadow, the shadow of my head, then scurries back, no connexion with me. Like a little creepy crawly it ventures out an instant, then goes back in again, the things one has to listen to, I say it as I hear it. It's the clerk's hand, is he entitled to the wig, I don't know, formerly perhaps. What do I do when silence falls, with rhetorical intent, or denoting lassitude, perplexity, consternation, I rub to and fro against my lips, where they meet, the first knuckle of my forefinger, but it's the head that moves, the hand rests, it's to such details the liar pins his hopes. That's the way this evening, tomorrow will be different, perhaps I'll appear before the council, before the justice of him who is all love, unforgiving and justly so, but subject to strange indulgences, the accused will be my soul, I prefer that, perhaps someone will ask pity for my soul, I musn't miss that, I won't be there, neither will God, it doesn't matter, we'll be represented. Yes, it can't be much longer now, I haven't been damned for what seems an eternity, yes, but sufficient unto the day, this evening I'm the scribe. This evening, it's always evening, always spoken of as evening, even when it's morning, it's to make me think night is at hand, bringer of rest. The first thing would be to believe I'm there, if I could do that I'd lap up the rest, there'd be none more credulous than me, if I were there. But I am, it's not possible otherwise, just so, it's not possible, it doesn't need to be possible. It's tiring, very tiring, in the same breath to win and lose, with concomitant emotions, one's heart is not of stone, to record the doom, don the black cap and collapse in the dock, very tiring, in the long run, I'm tired of it, I'd be tired of it, if I were me. It's a game, it's getting to be a game, I'm going to rise and go, if it's not me it will be someone, a phantom, long live all our phantoms, those of the dead, those of the living and those of those who are not born. I'll follow him, with my sealed eyes, he needs no door, needs no thought, to issue from this imaginary head, mingle with air and earth and dissolve, little by little, in exile. Now I'm haunted, let them go, one by one, let the last desert me and leave me empty, empty and silent. It's they murmur my name, speak to me of me, speak of a me, let them go and speak of it to others, who will not believe them either, or who will believe them too. Theirs all these voices, like a rattling of chains in my head, rattling to me that I have a head. That's where the court sits this evening, in the depths of that vaulty night, that's where I'm clerk and scribe, not understanding what I hear, not knowing what I write. That's where the council will be tomorrow, prayers will be offered for my soul, as for that of one dead, as for that of an infant dead in its dead mother, that it may not go to Limbo, sweet thing theology. It will be another evening, all happens at evening, but it will be the same night, it too has its evenings, its mornings and its evenings, there's a pretty conception, it's to make me think day is at hand, disperser of phantoms. And now birds, the first birds, what's this new trouble now, don't forget the question-mark. It must be the end of the session, it's been calm, on the whole. Yes, that's sometimes the way, there are suddenly birds and all goes silent, an instant. But the phantoms come back, it's in vain they go abroad, mingle with the dying, they come back and slip into the coffin, no bigger than a matchbox, it's they have taught me all I know, about things above, and all I'm said to know about me, they want to create me, they want to make me, like the bird the birdikin, with larvae she fetches from afar, at the peril—I nearly said at the peril of her life! But sufficient unto the day, those are other minutes. Yes, one begins to be very tired, very tired of one's toil, very tired of one's quill, it falls, it's noted.

# VI

How are the intervals filled between these apparitions? Do my keepers snatch a little rest and sleep before setting about me afresh, how would that be? That would be very natural, to enable them to get back their strength. Do they play cards, the odd rubber, bowls, to recruit their spirits, are they entitled to a little recreation? I would say no, if I had a say, no recreation, just a short break, with something cold, even though they should not feel inclined, in the interests of their health. They like their work, I feel it in my bones! No, I mean how filled for me, they don't come into this. Wretched acoustics this evening, the merest scraps, literally. The news, do you remember the news, the latest news, in slow letters of light, above Piccadilly Circus, in the fog? Where were you standing, in the doorway of the little tobacconist's closed for the night on the corner of Glasshouse Street was it, no, you don't remember, and for cause. Sometimes that's how it is, in a way, the eyes take over, and the silence, the sighs, like the sighs of sadness weary with crying, or old, that suddenly feels old and sighs for itself, for the happy days, the long days, when it cried it would never perish, but it's far from common, on the whole. My keepers, why keepers, I'm in no danger of stirring an inch, ah I see, it's to make me think I'm a prisoner, frantic with corporeality, rearing to get out and away. Other times it's male nurses, white from head to foot, even their shoes are white, and then it's another story, but the burden is the same. Other times it's like ghouls, naked and soft as worm, they grovel round me gloating on the corpse, but I have no more success dead than dying. Other times it's great clusters of bones, dangling and knocking with a clatter of castanets, it's clean and gay like coons, I'd join them with a will if it could be here and now, how is it nothing is ever here and now? It's varied, my life is varied, I'll never get anywhere. I know, there is no one here, neither me nor anyone else, but some things are better left unsaid, so I say nothing. Elsewhere perhaps, by all means, elsewhere, what elsewhere can there be to this infinite here? I know, if my head could think I'd find a way out, in my head, like so many others, and out of worse than this, the world would be there again, in my head, with me much as in the beginning. I would know that nothing had changed, that a little resolution is all that is needed to come and go under the changing sky, on the moving earth, as all along the long summer days too short for all the play, it was known as play, if my head could think. The air would be there again, the shadows of the sky drifting over the earth, and that ant, that ant, oh most excellent head that can't think. Leave it, leave it, nothing leads to anything, nothing of all that, my life is varied, you can't have everything, I'll never get anywhere, but when did I? When I laboured, all day long and let me add, before I forget, part of the night, when I thought that with perseverance I'd get at me in the end? Well look at me, a little dust in a little nook, stirred faintly this way and that by breath straying from the lost without. Yes, I'm here for ever, with the spinners and the dead flies, dancing to the tremor of their meshed wings, and it's well pleased I am, well pleased, that it's over and done with, the puffing and panting after me up and down their Tempe of tears. Sometimes a butterfly comes, all warm from the flowers, how weak it is, and quick dead, the wings crosswise, as when resting, in the sun, the scales grey. Blot, words can be blotted and the mad thoughts they invent, the nostalgia for that slime where the Eternal breathed and his son wrote, long after, with divine idiotic finger, at the feet of the adulteress, wipe it out, all you have to do is say you said nothing and so say nothing again. What can have become then of the tissues I was, I can see them no more, feel them no more, flaunting and fluttering all about and inside me, pah they must be still on their old prowl somewhere, passing themselves off as me. Did I ever believe in them, did I ever believe I was there, somewhere in that ragbag, that's more the line, of inquiry, perhaps I'm still there, as large as life, merely convinced I'm not. The eyes, yes, if these memories are mine, I must have believed in them an instant, believed it was me I saw there dimly in the depths of their glades. I can see me still, with those of now, sealed this long time, staring with those of then, I must have been twelve, because of the glass, a round shaving-glass, double-faced, faithful and magnifying, staring into one of the others, the true ones, true then, and seeing me there, imagining I saw me there, lurking behind the bluey veils, staring back sightlessly, at the age of twelve, because of the glass, on its pivot, because of my father, if it was my father, in the bathroom, with its view of the sea, the lightships at night, the red harbour light, if these memories concern me, at the age of twelve, or at the age of forty, for the mirror remained, my father went but the mirror remained, in which he had so greatly changed, my mother did her hair in it, with twitching hands, in another house, with no view of the sea, with a view of the mountains, if it was my mother, what a refreshing whiff of life on earth. I was, I was, they say in Purgatory, in Hell too, admirable singulars, admirable assurance. Plunged in ice up to the nostrils, the eyelids caked with frozen tears, to fight all your battles o'er again, what tranquillity, and know there are no more emotions in store, no, I can't have heard aright. How many hours to go, before the next silence, they are not hours, it will not be silence, how many hours still, before the next silence? Ah to know for sure, to know that this thing has no end, this thing, this thing, this farrago of silence and words, of silence that is not silence and barely murmured words. Or to know it's life still, a form of life, ordained to end, as others ended and will end, till life ends, in all its forms. Words, mine was never more than that, than this pell-mell babel of silence and words, my viewless form described as ended, or to come, or still in progress, depending on the words, the moments, long may it last in that singular way. Apparitions, keepers, what childishness, and ghouls, to think I said ghouls, do I as much as know what they are, of course I don't, and how the intervals are filled, as if I didn't know, as if there were two things, some other thing besides this thing, what is it, this unnamable thing that I name and name and never wear out, and I call that words. It's because I haven't hit on the right ones, the killers, haven't yet heaved them up from that heart-burning glut of words, with what words shall I name my un-namable words? And yet I have high hopes, I give you my word, high hopes, that one day I may tell a story, hear a story, yet another, with men, kinds of men as in the days when I played all regardless or nearly, worked and played. But first stop talking and get on with your weeping, with eyes wide open that the precious liquid may spill freely, without burning the lids, or the crystalline humour, I forget, whatever it is it burns. Tears, that could be the tone, if they weren't so easy, the true tone and tenor at last. Besides not a tear, not one, I'd be in greater danger of mirth, if it wasn't so easy. No, grave, I'll be grave, I'll close my ears, close my mouth and be grave. And when they open again it may be to hear a story, tell a story, in the true sense of the words, the word hear, the word tell, the word story, I have high hopes, a little story, with living creatures coming and going on a habitable earth crammed with the dead, a brief story, with night and day coming and going above, if they stretch that far, the words that remain, and I've high hopes, I give you my word.

# VII

Did I try everything, ferret in every hold, secretly, silently, patiently, listening? I'm in earnest, as so often, I'd like to be sure I left no stone unturned before reporting me missing and giving up. In every hold, I mean in all those places where there was a chance of my being, where once I used to lurk, waiting for the hour to come when I might venture forth, tried and trusty places, that's all I meant when I said in every hold. Once, I mean in the days when I still could move, and feel myself moving, painfully, barely, but unquestionably changing position on the whole, the trees were witness, the sands, the air of the heights, the cobblestones. This tone is promising, it is more like that of old, of the days and nights when in spite of all I was calm, treading back and forth the futile road, knowing it short and easy seen from Sirius, and deadly calm at the heart of my frenzies. My question, I had a question, ah yes, did I try everything, I can see it still, but it's passing, lighter than air, like a cloud, in moonlight, before the skylight, before the moon, like the moon, before the skylight. No, in its own way, I know it well, the way of an evening shadow you follow with your eyes, thinking of something else, yes, that's it, the mind elsewhere, and the eyes too, if the truth were known, the eyes elsewhere too. Ah if there must be speech at least none from the heart, no, I have only one desire, if I have it still. But another thing, before the ones that matter, I have just time, if I make haste, in the trough of all this time just time. Another thing, I call that another thing, the old thing I keep on not saying till I'm sick and tired, revelling in the flying instants, I call that revelling, now's my chance and I talk of revelling, it won't come back in a hurry if I remember right, but come back it must with its riot of instants. It's not me in any case, I'm not talking of me, I've said it a million times, no point in apologizing again, for talking of me, when there's X, that paradigm of human kind, moving at will, complete with joys and sorrows, perhaps even a wife and brats, forbears most certainly, a carcass in God's image and a contemporary skull, but above all endowed with movement, that's what strikes you above all, with his likeness so easy to take and his so instructive soul, that really, no, to talk of oneself, when there's X, no, what a blessing I'm not talking of myself, enough vile parrot I'll kill you. And what if all this time I had not stirred hand or foot from the third class waiting-room of the South-Eastern Railway Terminus, I never dared wait first on a third class ticket, and were still there waiting to leave, for the south-east, the south rather, east lay the sea, all along the track, wondering where on earth to alight, or my mind absent, elsewhere. The last train went at twenty-three thirty, then they closed the station for the night. What thronging memories, that's to make me think I'm dead, I've said it a million times. But the same return, like the spokes of a turning wheel, always the same, and all alike, like spokes. And yet I wonder, whenever the hour returns when I have to wonder that, if the wheel in my head turns, I wonder, so given am I to thinking with my blood, or if it merely swings, like a balance-wheel in its case, a minute to and fro, seeing the immensity to measure and that heads are only wound up once, so given am I to thinking with my breath. But tut there I am far again from that terminus and its pretty neo-Doric colonnade, and far from that heap of flesh, rind, bones and bristles waiting to depart it knows not where, somewhere south, perhaps asleep, its ticket between finger and thumb for the sake of appearances, or let fall to the ground in the great limpness of sleep, perhaps dreaming it's in heaven, alit in heaven, or better still the dawn, waiting for the dawn and the joy of being able to say, I've the whole day before me, to go wrong, to go right, to calm down, to give up, I've nothing to fear, my ticket is valid for life. Is it there I came to a stop, is that me still waiting there, sitting up stiff and straight on the edge of the seat, knowing the dangers of laisser-aller, hands on thighs, ticket between finger and thumb, in that great room dim with the platform gloom as dispensed by the quarter-glass self-closing door, locked up in those shadows, it's there, it's me. In that case the night is long and singularly silent, for one who seems to remember the city sounds, confusedly, sunk now to a single sound, the impossible confused memory of a single confused sound, lasting all night, swelling, dying, but never for an instant broken by a silence the like of this deafening silence. Whence it should follow, but does not, that the third class waiting-room of the South-Eastern Railway Terminus must be struck from the list of places to visit, see above, centuries above, that this lump is no longer me and that search should be made elsewhere, unless it be abandoned, which is my feeling. But not so fast, all cities are not eternal, that of this pensum is perhaps among the dead, and the station in ruins where I sit waiting, erect and rigid, hands on thighs, the tip of the ticket between finger and thumb, for a train that will never come, never go, natureward, or for day to break behind the locked door, through the glass black with the dust of ruin. That is why one must not hasten to conclude, the risk of error is too great. And to search for me elsewhere, where life persists, and me there, whence all life has withdrawn, except mine, if I'm alive, no, it would be a loss of time. And personally, I hear it said, personally I have no more time to lose, and that that will be all for this evening, that night is at hand and the time come for me too to begin.

# VIII

Only the words break the silence, all other sounds
have ceased. If I were silent I'd hear nothing. But if
I were silent the other sounds would start again, those
to which the words have made me deaf, or which have
really ceased. But I am silent, it sometimes happens,
no, never, not one second. I weep too without inter-
ruption. It's an unbroken flow of words and tears.
With no pause for reflection. But I speak softer, every
year a little softer. Perhaps. Slower too, every year a
little slower. Perhaps. It is hard for me to judge. If so
the pauses would be longer, between the words, the
sentences, the syllables, the tears, I confuse them,
words and tears, my words are my tears, my eyes my
mouth. And I should hear, at every little pause, if it's
the silence I say when I say that only the words break
it. But nothing of the kind, that's not how it is, it's for
ever the same murmur, flowing unbroken, like a single
endless word and therefore meaningless, for it's the
end gives the meaning to words. What right have you
then, no, this time I see what I'm up to and put a stop
to it, saying, None, none. But get on with the stupid
old threne and ask, ask until you answer, a new question, the most ancient of all, the question were things
always so. Well I'm going to tell myself something
(if I'm able), pregnant I hope with promise for the
future, namely that I begin to have no very clear
recollection of how things were before (I was!), and
by before I mean elsewhere, time has turned into space

and there will be no more time, till I get out of here. Yes, my past has thrown me out, its gates have slammed behind me, or I burrowed my way out alone, to linger a moment free in a dream of days and nights, dreaming of me moving, season after season, towards the last, like the living, till suddenly I was here, all memory gone. Ever since nothing but fantasies and hope of a story for me somehow, of having come from somewhere and of being able to go back, or on, somehow, some day, or without hope. Without what hope, haven't I just said, of seeing me alive, not merely inside an imaginary head, but a pebble sand to be, under a restless sky, restless on its shore, faint stirs day and night, as if to grow less could help, ever less and less and never quite be gone. No truly, no matter what, I say no matter what, hoping to wear out a voice, to wear out a head, or without hope, without reason, no matter what, without reason. But it will end, a desinence will come, or the breath fail better still, I'll be silence, I'll know I'm silence, no, in the silence you can't know, I'll never know anything. But at least get out of here, at least that, no? I don't know. And time begin again, the steps on the earth, the night the fool implores at morning and the morning he begs at evening not to dawn. I don't know, I don't know what all that means, day and night, earth and sky, begging and imploring. And I can desire them? Who says I desire them, the voice, and that I can't desire anything, that looks like a contradiction, it may be for all I know. Me, here, if they could open, those little words, open and swallow me up, perhaps that is what has happened. If so let them open again and let me out, in the tumult of light that sealed my eyes, and of men, to try and be one again. Or if I'm guilty let me be forgiven and graciously authorized to expiate, coming

41

and going in passing time, every day a little purer, a little deader. The mistake I make is to try and think, even the way I do, such as I am I shouldn't be able, even the way I do. But whom can I have offended so grievously, to be punished in this inexplicable way, all is inexplicable, space and time, false and inexplicable, suffering and tears, and even the old convulsive cry, It's not me, it can't be me. But am I in pain, whether it's me or not, frankly now, is there pain? Now is here and here there is no frankness, all I say will be false and to begin with not said by me, here I'm a mere ventriloquist's dummy, I feel nothing, say nothing, he holds me in his arms and moves my lips with a string, with a fish-hook, no, no need of lips, all is dark, there is no one, what's the matter with my head, I must have left it in Ireland, in a saloon, it must be there still, lying on the bar, it's all it deserved. But that other who is me, blind and deaf and mute, because of whom I'm here, in this black silence, helpless to move or accept this voice as mine, it's as him I must disguise myself till I die, for him in the meantime do my best not to live, in this pseudo-sepulture claiming to be his. Whereas to my certain knowledge I'm dead and kicking above, somewhere in Europe probably, with every plunge and suck of the sky a little more overripe, as yesterday in the pump of the womb. No, to have said so convinces me of the contrary, I never saw the light of day, any more than he, ah if no were content to cut yes's throat and never cut its own. Watch out for the right moment, then not another word, is that the only way to have being and habitat? But I'm here, that much at least is certain, it's in vain I keep on saying it, it remains true. Does it? It's hard for me to judge. Less true and less certain in any case than when I say I'm on earth, come into the

42

world and assured of getting out, that's why I say it, patiently, variously, trying to vary, for you never know, it's perhaps all a question of hitting on the right aggregate. So as to be here no more at last, to have never been here, but all this time above, with a name like a dog to be called up with and distinctive marks to be had up with, the chest expanding and contracting unaided, panting towards the grand apnoea. The right aggregate, but there are four million possible, nay probable, according to Aristotle, who knew everything. But what is this I see, and how, a white stick and an ear-trumpet, where, Place de la République, at pernod time, let me look closer at this, it's perhaps me at last. The trumpet, sailing at ear level, suddenly resembles a steam-whistle, of the kind thanks to which my steamers forge fearfully through the fog. That should fix the period, to the nearest half-century or so. The stick gains ground, tapping with its ferrule the noble bassamento of the United Stores, it must be winter, at least not summer. I can also just discern, with a final effort of will, a bowler hat which seems to my sorrow a sardonic synthesis of all those that never fitted me and, at the other extremity, similarly suspicious, a complete pair of brown boots lacerated and gaping. These insignia, if I may so describe them, advance in concert, as though connected by the traditional human excipient, halt, move on again, confirmed by the vast show windows. The level of the hat, and consequently of the trumpet, hold out some hope for me as a dying dwarf or at least hunchback. The vacancy is tempting, shall I enthrone my infirmities, give them this chance again, my dream infirmities, that they may take flesh and move, deteriorating, round and round this grandiose square which I hope I don't confuse with the Bastille, until they are deemed worthy of the adjacent Père Lachaise or, better still, prematurely relieved trying to cross over, at the hour of night's young thoughts. No, the answer is no. For even as I moved, or when the moment came, affecting beyond all others, to hold out my hand, or hat, without previous song, or any other form of concession to self-respect, at the terrace of a café, or in the mouth of the underground, I would know it was not me, I would know I was here, begging in another dark, another silence, for another alm, that of being or of ceasing, better still, before having been. And the hand old in vain would drop the mite and the old feet shuffle on, towards an even vainer death than no matter whose.

# IX

If I said, There's a way out there, there's a way out somewhere, the rest would come. What am I waiting for then, to say it? To believe it? And what does that mean, the rest? Shall I answer, try to answer, or go on as though I had asked nothing? I don't know, I can't know beforehand, nor after, nor during, the future will tell, some future instant, soon, or late, I won't hear, I won't understand, all dies so fast, no sooner born. And the yeses and noes mean nothing in this mouth, no more than sighs it sighs in its toil, or answers to a question not understood, a question unspoken, in the eyes of a mute, an idiot, who doesn't understand, never understood, who stares at himself in a glass, stares before him in the desert, sighing yes, sighing no, on and off. But there is reasoning somewhere, moments of reasoning, that is to say the same things recur, they drive one another out, they draw one another back, no need to know what things. It's mechanical, like the great colds, the great heats, the long days, the long nights, of the moon, such is my conviction, for I have convictions, when their turn comes round, then stop having them, that's how it goes, it must be supposed, at least it must be said, since I have just said it. The way out, this evening it's the turn of the way out, isn't it like a duo, or a trio, yes, there are moments when it's like that, then they pass and it's not like that any more, never was like that, is like nothing, no resemblance with anything, of no interest. What variety and at the same time what monotony, how varied it is and at the same time how, what's the word, how monotonous. What agitation and at the same time what calm, what vicissitudes within what changelessness. Moments of hesitation not so much rare as frequent, if one had to choose, and soon overcome in favour of the old crux, on which at first all depends, then much, then little, then nothing. That's right, wordshit, bury me, avalanche, and let there be no more talk of any creature, nor of a world to leave, nor of a world to reach, in order to have done, with worlds, with creatures, with words, with misery, misery. Which no sooner said, Ah, says I, punctually, if only I could say, There's a way out there, there's a way out somewhere, then all would be said, it would be the first step on the long travelable road, destination tomb, to be trod without a word, tramp tramp, little heavy irrevocable steps, down the long tunnels at first, then under the mortal skies, through the days and nights, faster and faster, no, slower and slower, for obvious reasons, and at the same time faster and faster, for other obvious reasons, or the same, obvious in a different way, or in the same way, but at a different moment of time, a moment earlier, a moment later, or at the same moment, there is no such thing, there would be no such thing, I recapitulate, impossible. Would I know where I came from, no, I'd have a mother, I'd have had a mother, and what I came out of, with what pain, no, I'd have forgotten, what is it makes me say that, what is it makes me say this, whatever it is makes me say all, and it's not certain, not certain the way the mother would be certain, the way the tomb would be certain, if there was a way out, if I said there was a way out, make me say it, demons, no, I'll ask for nothing. Yes, I'd

46

have a mother, I'd have a tomb, I wouldn't have come out of here, one doesn't come out of here, here are my tomb and mother, it's all here this evening, I'm dead and getting born, without having ended, helpless to begin, that's my life. How reasonable it is and what am I complaining of? Is it because I'm no longer slinking to and fro before the graveyard, saying, God grant I'm buriable before the curtain drops, is that my grievance, it's possible. I was well inspired to be anxious, wondering on what score, and I asked myself, as I came and went, on what score I could possibly be anxious, and found the answer and answered, saying, It's not me, I haven't yet appeared, I haven't yet been noticed, and saying further, Oh yes it is, it's me all right, and ceasing to be what is more, then quickening my step, so as to arrive before the next onslaught, as though it were on time I trod, and saying further, and so forth. I can scarcely have gone unperceived, all this time, and yet you wouldn't have thought so, that I didn't go unperceived. I don't refer to the spoken salutation, I'd have been the first to be perturbed by that, almost as much as by the bow, kiss or handshake. But the other signs, irrepressible, with which the fellow-creature unwillingly betrays your presence, the shudders and wry faces, nothing of that nature either it would seem, except possibly on the part of certain hearse-horses, in spite of their blinkers and strict funereal training, but perhaps I flatter myself. Truly I can't recall a single face, proof positive that I was not there, no, proof of nothing. But the fact that I was not molested, can I have remained insensible to that? Alas I fear they could have subjected me to the most gratifying brutalities, I won't go so far as to say without my knowledge, but without my being encouraged, as a result, to feel myself there rather than elsewhere. And I may well have spent one half of my life in the prisons of their Arcady, purging the delinquencies of the other half, all unaware of any break or lull in my problematic patrolling, unconstrained, before the gates of the graveyard. But what if weary of seeing me relieve myself, of seeing me resume, after each forced vacation, my beat before the gates of the graveyard, what if finally they had plucked up heart and slightly stressed their blows, just enough to confer death, without any mutilation of the corpse, there, at the gates of the graveyard, where that very morning I had reappeared, no sooner set at large, and resumed my old offence, to and fro, with step now slow and now precipitate, like that of the conspirator Catilina plotting the ruin of the fatherland, saying, It's not me, yes, it's me, and further, There's a way out there, no no, I'm getting mixed, I must be getting mixed, confusing here and there, now and then, just as I confused them then, the here of then, the then of there, with other spaces, other times, dimly discerned, but not more dimly than now, now that I'm here, if I'm here, and no longer there, coming and going before the graveyard, perplexed. Or did I end up by simply sitting down, with my back to the wall, all the long night before me when the dead lie waiting, on the beds where they died, shrouded or coffined, for the sun to rise? What am I doing now, I'm trying to see where I am, so as to be able to go elsewhere, should occasion arise, or else simply to say, You have merely to wait till they come and fetch you, that's my impression at times. Then it goes and I see it's not that, but something else, difficult to grasp, and which I don't grasp, or which I do grasp, it depends, and it comes to the same, for it's not that either, but something else, some other thing, or the first back again, or still the same, always the same thing proposing itself to my perplexity, then disappearing, then proposing itself again, to my perplexity still unsated, or momentarily dead, of starvation. The graveyard, yes, it's there I'd return, this evening it's there, borne by my words, if I could get out of here, that is to say if I could say, There's a way out there, there's a way out somewhere, to know exactly where would be a mere matter of time, and patience, and sequency of thought, and felicity of expression. But the body, to get there with, where's the body? It's a minor point, a minor point. And I have no doubts, I'd get there somehow, to the way out, sooner or later, if I could say, There's a way out there, there's a way out somewhere, the rest would come, the other words, sooner or later, and the power to get there, and the way to get there, and pass out, and see the beauties of the skies, and see the stars again.

# X

Give up, but it's all given up, it's nothing new, I'm nothing new. Ah so there was something once, I had something once. It may be thought there was, so long as it's known there was not, never anything, but giving up. But let us suppose there was not, that is to say let us suppose there was, something once, in a head, in a heart, in a hand, before all opened, emptied, shut again and froze. This is most reassuring, after such a fright, and emboldens me to go on, once again. But there is not silence. No, there is utterance, somewhere someone is uttering. Inanities, agreed, but is that enough, is that enough, to make sense? I see what it is, the head has fallen behind, all the rest has gone on, the head and its anus the mouth, or else it has gone on alone, all alone on its old prowls, slobbering its shit and lapping it back off the lips like in the days when it fancied itself. But the heart's not in it any more, nor is the appetite what it was. So home to roost it comes among my other assets, home yet again, and no trickery involved, that old past ever new, ever ended, ever ending, with all its hidden treasures of promise for tomorrow, and of consolation for today. And I'm in good hands again, they hold my head from behind, intriguing detail, as at the hairdresser's, the forefingers close my eyes, the middle fingers my nostrils, the thumbs stop up my ears, but imperfectly, to enable me to hear, but imperfectly, while the four remaining make merry with my jaws and tongue, to enable me to suffocate, but imperfectly, and to utter, for my good, what I must utter, for my future good, well-known ditty, and in particular to observe without delay, speaking of the passing moment, that worse have been known to pass, that it will pass in time, a mere moment of respite which but for this first aid might have proved fatal, and that one day I shall know again that I once was, and roughly who, and how to go on, and speak unaided, nicely, about number one and his pale imitations. And it is possible, just, for I must not be too affirmative at this stage, it would not be in my interest, that other fingers, quite a different gang, other tentacles, that's more like it, other charitable suckers, waste no more time trying to get it right, will take down my declarations, so that at the close of the interminable delirium, should it ever resume, I may not be reproached with having faltered. This is awful, awful, at least there's that to be thankful for. And perhaps beside me, and all around, other souls are being licked into shape, souls swooned away, or sick with over-use, or because no use could be found for them, but still fit for use, or fit only to be cast away, pale imitations of mine. Or has it knelled here at last for our committal to flesh, as the dead are committed to the ground, in the hour of their death at last, and at the place where they die, to keep the expenses down, or for our reassignment, souls of the stillborn, or dead before the body, or still young in the midst of the ruins, or never come to life through incapacity or for some other reason, or the immortal type, there must be a few of them too, whose bodies were always wrong, but patience there's a true one in pickle, among the unborn hordes, the true sepulchral body, for the living have no room for a second. No, no souls, or bodies, or birth, or life, or death, you've got to go on without any of that junk, that's all dead with words, with excess of words, they can say nothing else, they say there is nothing else, that here it's that and nothing else, but they won't say it eternally, they'll find some other nonsense, no matter what, and I'll be able to go on, no, I'll be able to stop, or start, another guzzle of lies but piping hot, it will last my time, it will be my time and place, my voice and silence, a voice of silence, the voice of my silence. It's with such prospects they exhort you to have patience, whereas you are patient, and calm, somehow some-where calm, what calm here, ah that's an idea, say how calm it is here, and how fine I feel, and how silent I am, I'll start right away, I'll say what calm and silence, which nothing has ever broken, nothing will ever break, which saying I don't break, or saying I'll be saying, yes, I'll say all that tomorrow, yes, tomorrow evening, some other evening, not this evening, this evening it's too late, too late to get things right, I'll go to sleep, so that I may say, hear myself say, a little later, I've slept, he's slept, but he won't have slept, or else he's sleeping now, he'll have done nothing, nothing but go on, doing what, doing what he does, that is to say, I don't know, giving up, that's it, I'll have gone on giving up, having had nothing, not being there.

# XI

When I think, no, that won't work, when come
those who knew me, perhaps even know me still, by
sight of course, or by smell, it's as though, it's as if,
come on, I don't know, I shouldn't have begun. If I
began again, setting my mind to it, that sometimes
gives good results, it's worth trying, I'll try it, one
of these days, one of these evenings, or this evening,
why not this evening, before I disappear, from up
there, from down here, scattered by the everlasting
words. What am I saying, scattered, isn't that just what
I'm not, just what I'm not, I was wandering, my mind
was wandering, just the very thing I'm not. And it's
still the same old road I'm trudging, up yes and
down no, towards one yet to be named, so that he
may leave me in peace, be in peace, be no more, have
never been. Name, no, nothing is namable, tell, no,
nothing can be told, what then, I don't know, I
shouldn't have begun. Add him to the repertory,
there we have it, and execute him, as I execute me,
one dead bar after another, evening after evening,
and night after night, and all through the days, but
it's always evening, why is that, why is it always
evening, I'll say why, so as to have said it, have it
behind me, an instant. It's time that can't go on at
the hour of the serenade, unless it's dawn, no, I'm not
in the open, I'm under the ground, or in my body
somewhere, or in another body, and time devours on,
but not me, there we have it, that's why it's always

evening, to let me have the best to look forward to, the long black night to sleep in, there, I've answered, I've answered something. Or it's in the head, like a minute time switch, a second time switch, or it's like a patch of sea, under the passing lighthouse beam, a passing patch of sea under the passing beam. Vile words to make me believe I'm here, and that I have a head, and a voice, a head believing this, then that, then nothing more, neither in itself, nor in anything else, but a head with a voice belonging to it, or to others, other heads, as if there were two heads, as if there were one head, or headless, a headless voice, but a voice. But I'm not deceived, for the moment I'm not deceived, for the moment I'm not there, nor anywhere else what is more, neither as head, nor as voice, nor as testicle, what a shame, what a shame I'm not appearing anywhere as testicle, or as cunt, those areas, a female pubic hair, it sees great sights, peeping down, well, there it is, can't be helped, that's how it is. And I let them say their say, my words not said by me, me that word, that word they say, but say in vain. We're getting on, getting on, and when come those who knew me, quick quick, it's as though, no, premature. But peekaboo here I come again, just when most needed, like the square root of minus one, having terminated my humanities, this should be worth seeing, the livid face stained with ink and jam, caput mortuum of a studious youth, ears akimbo, eyes back to front, the odd stray hair, foaming at the mouth, and chewing, what is it chewing, a gob, a prayer, a lesson, a little of each, a prayer got by rote in case of emergency before the soul resigns and bubbling up all arsy-varsy in the old mouth bereft of words, in the old head done with listening, there I am old, it doesn't take long, a snotty old nipper, having terminated his humanities, in the two-stander urinal on the corner of the Rue d'Assas was it, with the leak making the same gurgle as sixty years ago, my favourite because of the encouragement like mother hissing to baby on pot, my brow glued to the partition among the graffiti, straining against the prostate, belching up Hail Marys, buttoned as to the fly, I invent nothing, through absent-mindedness, or exhaustion, or insouciance, or on purpose, to promote priming, I know what I mean, or one-armed, better still, no arms, no hands, better by far, as old as the world and no less hideous, amputated on all sides, erect on my trusty stumps, bursting with old piss, old prayers, old lessons, soul, mind and carcass finishing neck and neck, not to mention the gobchucks, too painful to mention, sobs made mucus, hawked up from the heart, now I have a heart, now I'm complete, apart from a few extremities, having terminated their humanities, then their career, and with that not in the least pretentious, making no demands, rent with ejaculations, Jesus, Jesus. Evenings, evenings, what evenings they were then, made of what, and when was that, I don't know, made of friendly shadows, friendly skies, of time cloyed, resting from devouring, until its midnight meats, I don't know, any more than then, when I used to say, from within, or from without, from the coming night or from under the ground, Where am I, to mention only space, and in what semblance, and since when, to mention also time, and till when, and who is this clot who doesn't know where to go, who can't stop, who takes himself for me and for whom I take myself, anything at all, the old jangle. Those evenings then, but what is this evening made of, this evening now, that never ends, in whose shadows I'm alone, that's where I am, where I was then, where

I've always been, it's from them I spoke to myself, spoke to him, where has he vanished, the one I saw then, is he still in the street, it's probable, it's possible, with no voice speaking to him, I don't speak to him any more, I don't speak to me any more, I have no one left to speak to, and I speak, a voice speaks that can be none but mine, since there is none but me. Yes, I have lost him and he has lost me, lost from view, lost from hearing, that's what I wanted, is it possible, that I wanted that, wanted this, and he, what did he want, he wanted to stop, perhaps he has stopped, I have stopped, but I never stirred, perhaps he is dead, I am dead, but I never lived. But he moved, proof of animation, through those evenings, moving too, evenings with an end, evenings with a night, never saying a word, unable to say a word, not knowing where to go, unable to stop, listening to my cries, hearing a voice crying that it was no kind of life, as if he didn't know, as if the allusion was to his, which was a kind of one, there's the difference, those were the days, I didn't know where I was, nor in what semblance, nor since when, nor till when, whereas now, there's the difference, now I know, it's not true, but I say it just the same, there's the difference, I'm saying it now, I'll say it soon, I'll say it in the end, then end, I'll be free to end, I won't be any more, it won't be worth it any more, it won't be necessary any more, it won't be possible any more, but it's not worth it now, it's not necessary now, it's not possible now, that's how the reasoning runs. No, something better must be found, a better reason, for this to stop, another word, a better idea, to put in the negative, a new no, to cancel all the others, all the old noes that buried me down here, deep in this place which is not one, which is merely a moment for the time being eternal, which is called here, and in this being which is called me and is not one, and in this impossible voice, all the old noes dangling in the dark and swaying like a ladder of smoke, yes, a new no, that none says twice, whose drop will fall and let me down, shadow and babble, to an absence less vain than inexistence. Oh I know it won't happen like that, I know that nothing will happen, that nothing has happened and that I'm still, and particularly since the day I could no longer believe it, what is called flesh and blood somewhere above in their gonorrhoeal light, cursing myself heartily. And that is why, when comes the hour of those who knew me, this time it's going to work, when comes the hour of those who knew me, it's as though I were among them, that is what I had to say, among them watching me approach, then watching me recede, shaking my head and saying, Is it really he, can it possibly be he, then moving on in their company along a road that is not mine and with every step takes me further from that other not mine either, or remaining alone where I am, between two parting dreams, knowing none, known of none, that finally is what I had to say, that is all I can have had to say, this evening.

# XII

It's a winter night, where I was, where I'm going, remembered, imagined, no matter, believing in me, believing it's me, no, no need, so long as the others are there, where, in the world of the others, of the long mortal ways, under the sky, with a voice, no, no need, and the power to move, now and then, no need either, so long as the others move, the true others, but on earth, beyond all doubt on earth, for as long as it takes to die again, wake again, long enough for things to change here, for something to change, to make possible a deeper birth, a deeper death, or resurrection in and out of this murmur of memory and dream. A winter night, without moon or stars, but light, he sees his body, all the front, part of the front, what makes them light, this impossible night, this impossible body, it's me in him remembering, remembering the true night, dreaming of the night without morning, and how will he manage tomorrow, to endure tomorrow, the dawning, then the day, the same as he managed yesterday, to endure yesterday. Oh I know, it's not me, not yet, it's a veteran, inured to days and nights, but he forgets, he thinks of me, more than is wise, and it's a far cry to morning, perhaps it has time never to dawn at last. That's what he says, with his voice soon to leave him, perhaps tonight, and he says, How light it is, how shall I manage tomorrow, how did I manage yester- day, pah it's the end, it's a far cry to morning, and who's this speaking in me, and who's this disowning me, as though I had taken his place, usurped his life, that old shame that kept me from living, the shame of my living that kept me from living, and so on, muttering, the old inanities, his chin on his heart, his arms dangling, sagging at the knees, in the night. Will they succeed in slipping me into him, the memory and dream of me, into him still living, amn't I there already, wasn't I always there, like a stain of remorse, is that my night and contumacy, in the dungeons of this moribund, and from now till he dies my last chance to have been, and who is this raving now, pah there are voices everywhere, ears everywhere, one who speaks saying, without ceasing to speak, Who's speaking?, and one who hears, mute, uncomprehending, far from all, and bodies everywhere, bent, fixed, where my prospects must be just as good, just as poor, as in this firstcomer. And none will wait, he no more than the others, none ever waited to die for me to live in him, so as to die with him, but quick quick all die, saying, Quick quick let us die, without him, as we lived, before it's too late, lest we won't have lived. And this other now, obviously, what's to be said of this latest other, with his babble of homeless mes and untenanted hims, this other without number or person whose abandoned being we haunt, nothing. There's a pretty three in one, and what a one, what a no one. So, I'm supposed to say now, it's the moment, so that's the earth, these expiring vitals set aside for me which no sooner taken over would be set aside for another, many thanks, and here the laugh, the long silent guffaw of the knowing non-exister, at hearing ascribed to him such pregnant words, confess you're not the man you were, you'll end up riding a bicycle. That's the accountants' chorus, opining like a single man, and there are more to come, all the peoples of the earth would not suffice, at the end of the billions you'd need a god, unwitnessed witness of witnesses, what a blessing it's all down the drain, nothing ever as much as begun, nothing ever but nothing and never, nothing ever but lifeless words.

# XIII

Weaker still the weak old voice that tried in vain to make me, dying away as much as to say it's going from here to try elsewhere, or dying down, there's no telling, as much as to say it's going to cease, give up trying. No voice ever but it in my life, it says, if speaking of me one can speak of life, and it can, it still can, or if not of life, there it dies, if this, if that, if speaking of me, there it dies, but who can the greater can the less, once you've spoken of me you can speak of anything, up to the point where, up to the time when, there it dies, it can't go on, it's been its death, speaking of me, here or elsewhere, it says, it murmurs. Whose voice, no one's, there is no one, there's a voice without a mouth, and somewhere a kind of hearing, something compelled to hear, and somewhere a hand, it calls that a hand, it wants to make a hand, or if not a hand something somewhere that can leave a trace, of what is made, of what is said, you can't do with less, no, that's romancing, more romancing, there is nothing but a voice murmuring a trace. A trace, it wants to leave a trace, yes, like air leaves among the leaves, among the grass, among the sand, it's with that it would make a life, but soon it will be the end, it won't be long now, there won't be any life, there won't have been any life, there will be silence, the air quite still that trembled once an instant, the tiny flurry of dust quite settled. Air, dust, there is no air here, nor anything to make dust, and to speak of instants, to speak of once, is to speak of nothing, but there it is, those are the expressions it employs. It has always spoken, it will always speak, of things that don't exist, or only exist elsewhere, if you like, if you must, if that may be called existing. Unfortunately it is not a question of elsewhere, but of here, ah there are the words out at last, out again, that was the only chance, get out of here and go elsewhere, go where time passes and atoms assemble an instant, where the voice belongs perhaps, where it sometimes says it must have belonged, to be able to speak of such figments. Yes, out of here, but how when here is empty, not a speck of dust, not a breath, the voice's breath alone, it breathes in vain, nothing is made. If I were here, if it could have made me, how I would pity it, for having spoken so long in vain, no, that won't do, it wouldn't have spoken in vain if I were here, and I wouldn't pity it if it had made me, I'd curse it, or bless it, it would be in my mouth, cursing, blessing, whom, what, it wouldn't be able to say, in my mouth it wouldn't have much to say, that had so much to say in vain. But this pity, all the same, it wonders, this pity that is in the air, though no air here for pity, but it's the expression, it wonders should it stop and wonder what pity is doing here and if it's not hope gleaming, another expression, evilly among the imaginary ashes, the faint hope of a faint being after all, human in kind, tears in its eyes before they've had time to open, no, no more stopping and wondering, about that or anything else, nothing will stop it any more, in its fall, or in its rise, perhaps it will end on a castrato scream. True there was never much talk of the heart, literal or figurative, but that's no reason for hoping, what, that one day there will be one, to send up above to break in the galanty show, pity. But

62

what more is it waiting for now, when there's no doubt left, no choice left, to stick a sock in its death-rattle, yet another locution. To have rounded off its cock-and-bullshit in a coda worthy of the rest? Last everlasting questions, infant languors in the end sheets, last images, end of dream, of being past, passing and to be, end of lie. Is it possible, is that the possible thing at last, the extinction of this black nothing and its impossible shades, the end of the farce of making and the silencing of silence, it wonders, that voice which is silence, or it's me, there's no telling, it's all the same dream, the same silence, it and me, it and him, him and me, and all our train, and all theirs, and all theirs, but whose, whose dream, whose silence, old questions, last questions, ours who are dream and silence, but it's ended, we're ended who never were, soon there will be nothing where there was never anything, last images. And whose the shame, at every mute micro-millisyllable, and unshakable infinity of remorse delving ever deeper in its bite, at having to hear, having to say, fainter than the faintest murmur, so many lies, so many times the same lie lyingly denied, whose the screaming silence of no's knife in yes's wound, it wonders. And wonders what has become of the wish to know, it is gone, the heart is gone, the head is gone, no one feels anything, asks anything, seeks anything, says anything, hears anything, there is only silence. It's not true, yes, it's true, it's true and it's not true, there is silence and there is not silence, there is no one and there is someone, nothing prevents anything. And were the voice to cease quite at last, the old ceasing voice, it would not be true, as it is not true that it speaks, it can't speak, it can't cease. And were there one day to be here, where there are no days, which is no place, born of the impossible voice the unmakable being, and a gleam of light, still all would be silent and empty and dark, as now, as soon now, when all will be ended, all said, it says, it murmurs.